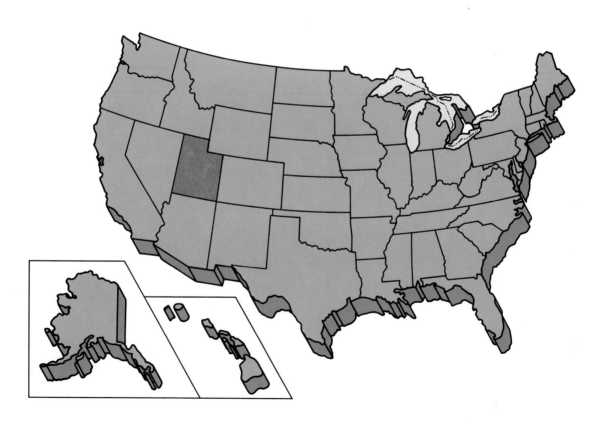

UTAH

# UTAH

## Karen Sirvaitis

Lerner Publications Company

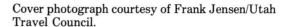

Cover photograph courtesy of Frank Jensen/Utah Travel Council.

The glossary that begins on page 68 gives definitions of words shown in **bold type** in the text.

LIBRARY OF CONGRESS
CATALOGING-IN-PUBLICATION DATA
Sirvaitis, Karen.
    Utah / Karen Sirvaitis.
       p.    cm. — (Hello USA)
    Includes index.
    Summary: Introduces the geography, history, industries, people, and other highlights of Utah.
    ISBN 0-8225-2707-3 (lib. bdg.)
    1. Utah—Juvenile literature.
  [1. Utah.] I. Title. II. Series.
F826.3.S58  1991
979.2—dc20           90-13535
                    CIP
                    AC

# CONTENTS

**Sea gulls soar over Great Salt Lake.**

# Did You Know...?

❑ Utahns named the sea gull their state bird because the insect-eaters saved crops from an invasion of crickets in 1848. The Sea Gull Monument in Salt Lake City is dedicated to the bird.

❑ The symbol for Paramount Pictures, a major motion-picture company, features Mt. Ben Lomond, a mountain peak near Ogden.

❑ On May 10, 1869, at Promontory in northern Utah, workers laid the last piece of railroad track necessary to join the East Coast with the West Coast.

❑ A place in Utah allows cars to travel 600 miles (960 kilometers) per hour! At Bonneville Salt Flats International Speedway, located near Wendover, many car-racing records have been set.

❑ Great Salt Lake, in northern Utah, has been as much as eight times saltier than any of the oceans. Swimmers can float easily in the salt-heavy water.

The sego lily is the state flower of Utah.

# A Trip Around the State

Salty lakes, goblin-shaped rocks, dinosaur graveyards. Many Utahns would say a varied landscape is part of what makes their state unique. Snowcapped mountain peaks may overlook miles of **desert** in one place, while close by may be a mighty river, a deep **canyon,** or a fertile valley.

Three land regions—the Great Basin, the Rocky Mountain, and the Colorado Plateau—define Utah.

**Jagged rocks rise from Bryce Canyon, in southern Utah.**

The sandstone walls of Dinosaur National Monument contain thousands of dinosaur bones that have turned to fossils.

The Great Basin region covers western Utah from north to south. Although it is a desert and one of the driest areas of the nation, the Great Basin includes Utah's largest body of water, Great Salt Lake. Its water is unusual because it is very salty—saltier than any of the oceans. For this reason, the lake is called an **inland sea**.

Spanning 2,000 square miles (5,180 sq km), Great Salt Lake is what remains of a much larger ancient lake that scientists call Bonneville. Thousands of years ago, Lake Bonneville covered much of the Great Basin. Over time, most of the water dried up, leaving Great Salt Lake and a broad stretch of **salt flats** that are packed as hard as concrete.

Utah lies in the western United States midway between Mexico and Canada. Because ranges of the Rocky Mountains pass through Utah, it is considered a Rocky Mountain state. Utah borders six other states. They are Nevada, Idaho, Wyoming, Colorado, New Mexico, and Arizona.

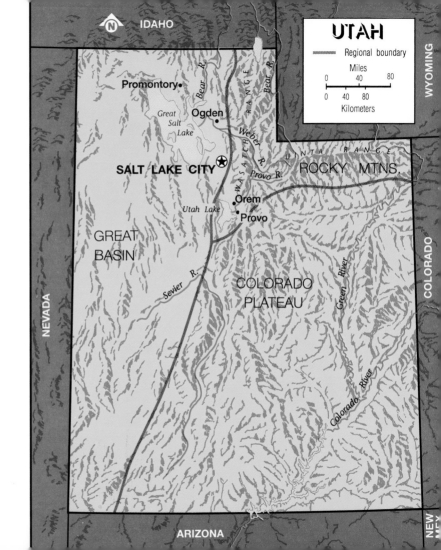

During the winter, snow covers the Wasatch Range.

Another special feature of the state is the Uinta Range in the Rocky Mountain region of northeastern Utah. The Rockies, a nickname for the Rocky Mountains, span parts of the western United States and Canada. Of all the ranges included in this chain of mountains, only the Uinta extends west to east. Other ranges of the Rockies, including the Wasatch in Utah, run north to south.

A coyote pauses near a mountain stream.

The Colorado Plateau stretches across most of southern and eastern Utah. The **plateau,** a broad expanse of high land, is hard and rocky. Rivers have carved deep canyons in this region, most of which is too rugged for growing crops. Over millions of years, wind and rain have sculpted rocks on the plateau into strange shapes, some of which look like castles, ships, and goblins.

The Colorado River flows through the Colorado Plateau. The Colorado and its main **tributary,** the Green River, are major sources of waterpower for Utah.

The Bear, Provo, and Weber rivers begin in the Uinta Range. The Bear and Weber eventually drain into Great Salt Lake. The Provo empties into Utah Lake. The Sevier River is the longest waterway in southwestern Utah. Together these six rivers provide Utah with much of the water it needs for its farmlands, businesses, and households.

Even though it has many rivers, Utah is the second driest state in the country. (Nevada is the first.) Utah's deserts capture only about 5 inches (13 centimeters) of rain and snow each year, while the Rockies get at least 40 inches (102 cm). Summertime temperatures in the desert can soar above 100° F (38° C). During the winter, temperatures in the mountains often drop below freezing.

The Colorado River winds through Dead Horse Point State Park in eastern Utah.

The Joshua tree can grow to be 25 feet (8 meters) tall.

A variety of plants and animals live in Utah. Some like the dry desert heat, while others need the coolness of high mountain areas. Most trees, such as blue spruce, white balsam, and aspen, grow on and around the mountains. These trees cannot survive on the scarce water available in the desert sands.

Cactuses, sword plants, and sagebrush grow in the dry, rocky areas of the state. Southwestern Utah is home to the Joshua tree. This yucca is a tall, thick plant with white blossoms and some features of a tree. The Joshua tree got its name in the 1880s. A few people thought its limbs looked like arms lifted in prayer and called it Joshua, after a religious leader in the Bible.

Prairie dogs, bighorn sheep, buffalo, mountain lions, coyotes, foxes, and beavers are among the many mammals that live in the state. Rattlesnakes are the only poisonous snakes found in Utah. Other reptiles include the desert tortoise and the Gila monster, the only poisonous lizard in the state.

**The slow-moving tortoise, or land turtle, crawls in Utah's deserts.**

**Aspens, which are found in northern Utah, display golden leaves each fall.**

# Utah's Story

Long before the United States existed, many groups of Indians lived throughout the North American continent. As long as 12,000 years ago, small bands of Indians roamed the area now called Utah. For food they hunted animals and gathered wild berries, roots, and nuts.

Over time, the Indians began to grow their food. They planted corn and beans. They also continued to hunt. These early Indians are called the Basket Makers because they crafted baskets, ropes, and sandals from dried grasses. The Basket Makers also made nets for catching small animals.

Eventually, the Basket Makers discovered how to channel water from rivers to their fields, a practice called **irrigation**. The crops produced plenty of food for the Indians.

As their farming skills improved, the Indians no longer needed to move from place to place to find their meals. Around A.D. 750, the Basket Makers began to build groups of permanent houses that were later called **pueblos,** the Spanish word for "villages." The people who built these villages eventually became known as Pueblo Indians.

To help shield themselves from enemies, the Pueblos later constructed homes on cliffside ledges.

**The Basket Makers probably ate the seeds, fruits, and stems of cactuses.**

**Ancient cliff dwellings built by Pueblo Indians still exist in the southwestern United States.**

But cliff dwellings could not protect the Indians completely. By 1300 the Pueblo Indians had disappeared from Utah, possibly because of attacks from more warlike Indians.

Rock carvings made by Indians can be found at Newspaper Rock State Park in southeastern Utah.

Tribes that spoke Shoshonean languages had entered the area by the time the Pueblos had disappeared. These groups—the Ute, the Paiutes, the Gosiutes, and the Shoshones—shared certain customs, but each had its own form of government. They moved from place to place, hunting deer and antelope and gathering plants. For centuries, the lifestyles of the Shoshonean-speaking peoples changed very little.

In 1776 two Spanish priests from Mexico, Francisco Atanasio Domínguez and Silvestre Vélez de Escalante, traveled through what is now Utah. After the priests' exploration, the Spanish claimed Utah for Spain, opening it up for white settlers.

Spain did not send many people to live in the newly claimed land and had very little contact with the Indians. People from other countries, however, began to take an interest in the Spanish territory. Throughout the early 1800s, fur trappers and explorers came to Utah from many dif-

**Escalante** *(right)*, **led by an Indian guide** *(left)*, **reached present-day Utah in 1776.**

ferent places. These people rarely crossed paths with the Indians.

In 1846 a group of people from Nauvoo, Illinois, began looking westward for a new home. Their decision to move to Utah eventually would have a major impact on the lives of the Indians.

At Nauvoo stood the Church of Jesus Christ of Latter-day Saints. The church's members, called Latter-day Saints, or Mormons, studied the Bible along with some of their own religious works. The church urged members to help each other and to work hard. In just a few years, the Mormons had established a large community in Nauvoo and had helped to make the city one of the wealthiest in Illinois.

Mormons were often treated unfairly because of their success and because they held some uncommon beliefs. One such belief was that a man could practice **polygyny**— that is, he could have more than one wife at a time. Fearing they might be in danger, the Mormons fled Nauvoo shortly after their church's founder, Joseph Smith, was killed by an angry mob of non-Mormons.

Brigham Young, the church's president, planned to take the Latter-day Saints to a place where they could follow their religion in peace. Late in 1846, about 150 Mormons, led by Brigham Young, headed west. Months later they arrived in Salt Lake Valley, near the site that would become Salt Lake City. The valley was dry and appeared to be uninhabited.

## Mormon Pioneers

Brigham Young *(right)* and the Mormon pioneers he led arrived in Salt Lake Valley on July 24, 1847. In the years that followed, thousands of Mormons from all over the world flocked to the valley. Most traveled in covered wagons, which were hard to control in the steep canyons. Those without wagons walked, pushing carts loaded with their belongings.

**The Ute Indians helped Mormon pioneers find enough food to eat until crops could be harvested.**

Ute Indians lived close to where the Mormons chose to settle. The Ute distrusted the newcomers at first, but soon the two groups got along well. The Indians taught the settlers which plants were safe to eat. Later, the Mormons gave the Indians food and clothing and preached the Mormon religion to some of them.

In 1847 Salt Lake Valley was part of Mexico, which had won its independence from Spain in 1821. At the close of the Mexican-American War (1846–1848), Mexico lost much of its northern territory—including the Mormons' new homeland—to the United States.

Meanwhile, the Mormons were planting crops in the best soils of Salt Lake Valley. Together they built homes, schools, and churches. They irrigated their crops with water from nearby rivers. By 1849 the Mormons had set up a government. They fixed boundaries for what they called the State of Deseret and chose Brigham Young as their governor.

The Mormons wanted Deseret to be admitted to the Union as the next state. Instead, the U.S. government made Deseret into the Territory of Utah (named after the Ute Indians). As a territory, Utah had fewer rights than did states. But the U.S. government had decided that until Mormon men stopped taking several wives, Utah would remain a territory.

When the Mormon church allowed the practice of polygyny, Mormon families were unusually large.

In 1849 someone in California hollered "Gold!" and the California gold rush began. For three years, thousands of miners stopped in Utah on their way to and from California. Tired, hungry, and sometimes rich, they were willing to pay the Mormons for food and fresh horses.

When business was good, some Mormons made a lot of money. Because Mormon church officials expected their followers to donate a **tithe** (10 percent of their income) to the church, the church was also getting rich.

From 1849 to 1852, people traveled across Utah on their way to California to pan for gold.

On their journeys to Salt Lake Valley, Mormons passed the Uinta Range.

The church often sent its members to other parts of the world to preach the Mormon gospel and to return with new believers. By 1852 more than 20,000 Mormons from all over the world had come to Utah. More and more, they settled in areas of Utah outside Salt Lake Valley.

The Indians were getting angry. The Mormons who were moving into other parts of the territory planted crops where wild berries had been growing. These Mormons built homes near streams and rivers where the Indians fished.

A Ute chief named Wakara, but called Walker by settlers, decided to take action. In 1853 Chief Wakara led the Indians against the white settlers in what became known as the Walker War. By the end of the war in 1854, the Ute had not won back any territory, and the Mormons continued to build settlements.

**Chief Wakara**

A few years after the Walker War, another war broke out in Utah. This time the fighting was between the Mormon church and the United States. The U.S. government had sent non-Mormon leaders to help govern the territory. These officials accused Mormons of ignoring the non-Mormon government. They said the Mormons turned instead to church officials for leadership.

The U.S. government sent troops to Utah in 1857, signaling the beginning of the Utah War (also called the Mormon War). Soon after the troops reached Utah, the Mormons agreed to let a non-Mormon govern the territory. The army stayed to discourage trouble.

The soldiers left in 1861, when they were needed to fight in the Civil War, the war between the Northern and the Southern states. Utah's government gathered a volunteer army to watch the Mormons and to keep the Ute from taking back any land from settlers. The leader of this army, Patrick Connor, often led attacks against the Indians.

# Mountain Meadows Massacre

On September 11, 1857, a party of 140 non-Mormon pioneers was camped in a meadow just 40 miles outside of Cedar City in southern Utah. Having traveled hundreds of miles from Arkansas, the men, women, and children were weary. The pioneers had many troubles along their journey. Food was scarce and the sun was blistering. The travelers probably felt that their problems could not get much worse.

Quite unexpectedly, a group of Mormon militiamen and some of their Indian friends attacked the wagon train, killing all but a few children. The attack became known as the Mountain Meadows Massacre. The Mormons claimed that the travelers were responsible for the death of Joseph Smith, founder of the Mormon religion. After investigations, only one person—an Indian farmer—was executed for the crime.

**Patrick Connor**

Patrick Connor disliked the Mormons as much as he disliked the Indians. He wanted more non-Mormons to live in Utah. He had his soldiers search for gold, silver, iron—any metal that would encourage non-Mormons to move to Utah. Hundreds of non-Mormon miners arrived. Some of them built the town of Corinne, the first white, non-Mormon city in Utah.

Miners who wanted to dig on Indian lands ended up battling Indians. To stop the fighting, the U.S. government and Connor's troops pressured the Indians into giving up their land.

The U.S. government set aside areas of land, called **reservations**, onto which the Indians of Utah were forced to move. No longer were they free to live throughout their native homeland.

Up until the mid-1800s, the Ute *(above)* often raided the Paiutes' villages *(right)*. The Ute kidnapped women and children and then sold them to other Indian groups as slaves.

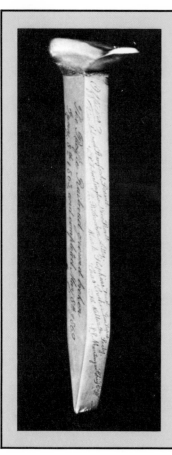

# The Golden Link

In 1869 the last link in America's first cross-country railroad was hammered into place in Utah. This feat connected the Atlantic and Pacific coasts. Trains soon carried people and goods across country faster than horses or oxen could, and travel between the two coasts increased. The original golden spike *(left)* used to connect the East with the West is on display at Union Station Museum in Ogden.

By the 1870s, the mining business in Utah was booming. Because the Mormon church at first discouraged its followers from working in the mines, mine owners asked people from places as far away as Greece, Finland, and Japan to work for their companies. **Immigrants** (newcomers), attracted by the jobs, came by the thousands. Utah's non-Mormon population grew rapidly.

Many of the territory's residents were eager to make Utah a state. But the Mormons' practice of polygyny was still a roadblock. In 1890 Mormon church officials agreed not to let a man have more than one wife, and in 1896 Utah became the 45th state in the Union.

Reed L. Smoot

As a state, Utah could send politicians to the nation's capital to speak on issues concerning the whole country. In 1903 Utahns elected Reed L. Smoot as a **senator.** Smoot's job involved working as a lawmaker and attending meetings of Congress.

Utahns worked hard to supply the U.S. military during World War II.

Smoot, however, was a Mormon, and U.S. government officials distrusted Mormons. Politicians believed Mormons were still practicing polygyny and that church leaders had too much say in Utah's government. Congress placed Smoot on trial, questioning him about his duties in the church. After several years in court, Congress had not cleared up all its concerns about Smoot but decided to let him represent Utah as a senator. He did so for 30 years.

Other conflicts that were much larger had good effects on Utah's economy during the first half of the 1900s. Mines in Utah furnished metals needed to make bullets and parts for planes, tanks, and guns used in World Wars I and II. These items earned a lot of money for the state.

Utah continued to make military equipment after the two world wars. Factories and test sites for rockets are on about 5 percent of Utah's land. These military sites are located on barren land, in areas where few people live.

Many rockets were tested in Utah in the late 1950s.

Bands of Indians
live in Utah

Basket Makers begin
building pueblos

Shoshonean-speaking
tribes enter the region

Utah's state flag became
official in 1913. The
yellow cone in the center
of the seal is a beehive,
which stands for
industry, or hard work.

40

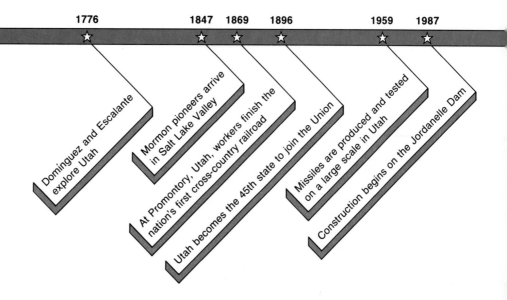

1776 — Dominguez and Escalante explore Utah

1847 — Mormon pioneers arrive in Salt Lake Valley

1869 — At Promontory, Utah, workers finish the nation's first cross-country railroad

1896 — Utah becomes the 45th state to join the Union

1959 — Missiles are produced and tested on a large scale in Utah

1987 — Construction begins on the Jordanelle Dam

Since the 1960s, workers have been building dams on Utah's rivers. When completed, the dams will supply more water to the state's growing urban areas. Changes like these are not always good for the land. But Utahns have been careful to preserve much of Utah's beauty.

41

# Living and Working in Utah

Many Utahns live and work in or near Salt Lake Valley, where Brigham Young first led the Mormons. Utah's population reached nearly 1.8 million in 1990. Large cities include Salt Lake City (Utah's capital), Provo, Ogden, and Orem. More than 85 percent of the state's population lives in northern Utah because most other parts of the state are so dry and rugged.

**Many Utahns live in Salt Lake City** *(above)*, **the state's capital and largest city. A small number of people farm Utah's rural areas** *(facing page).*

Almost everyone living in Utah was born in the United States. Most of Utah's recent immigrants have come from Germany, Canada, Great Britain, or Mexico. Blacks, some of whom are descended from slaves brought by the first Mormons, make up less than 1 percent of Utah's population.

Indians, who once were the only people in Utah, now number less than 1 percent. Most of the Ute live on the Uintah and Ouray Reservation near the Uinta Range. During the 1980s, leaders from this reservation created more jobs for the Ute. Their most successful businesses include a cattle ranch and a motel and recreational center. The Paiutes and the

Utah has a large population of young people.

Gosiutes have smaller reservations elsewhere in the state.

The Navajo Reservation, the largest Indian reservation in the country, extends from Arizona and New Mexico up into southeastern Utah. Nearly half of Utah's Indians live on this reservation.

A Navajo woman weaves a rug in her home in Monument Valley. Many of Utah's Navajo Indians live on a reservation in southeastern Utah.

**Mormons completed Salt Lake Temple in 1893. Construction of the temple took 40 years.**

Seventy percent of all Utahns belong to the Church of Jesus Christ of Latter-day Saints. The Salt Lake Temple in Salt Lake City is the world headquarters for the church. Mormons are still expected to donate 10 percent of their income to the church.

A high school student in Utah conducts a chemistry experiment.

Utah has earned the highest **literacy rate,** a measure of how many people can read and write, in the nation. Classroom education in Utah began when Mormons set up a school in 1847, shortly after coming to Salt Lake Valley. They pitched a tent that served as a classroom. The first public school opened in 1866.

The Mormon church encourages its members to trace their family roots as far back as possible. The church even has a special library that stores the records people need to chart their family trees. Called the Family History Library, it has one of the world's largest collections of such records.

Utah's Ballet West is considered one of the top dance companies in the United States.

Surrounded by mountains and deserts, Salt Lake City is the largest cultural center for miles around. The Utah Symphony performs in the modern Symphony Hall. The Utah Opera Company and Ballet West entertain audiences in the historic Capitol Theatre. Accompanied by a bellowing pipe organ, the 325-member Mormon Tabernacle Choir sings in the Salt Lake Tabernacle, a place of worship.

Utah's wilderness lends itself to many sporting activities. Its snow-covered mountain slopes attract downhill skiers. Its rivers, pounding against underwater rocks, are ideal for white-water rafting.

Each year thousands of campers, hikers, and horseback riders tour Utah's canyons. Arches, Bryce Canyon, Canyonlands, Capitol Reef, and Zion are the national parks in Utah, where thousands of acres are set aside as wilderness areas.

Many of the outdoor enthusiasts in Utah are tourists. The state earns about $1 billion each year from visitors. Workers who serve these tourists have service jobs.

Other Utahns who make a living helping people include teachers, doctors, salesclerks, bankers, and the governor. More Utahns work in education than in any other service field. About 75 percent of Utah's work force, including those who work in government, holds some type of service job.

**Campers ride horses along a creek in Canyonlands National Park.**

At Bingham Canyon, miners remove copper ore from the surface of the steps. Each step is 40 to 70 feet (12 to 21 m) high.

Manufacturing employs 15 percent of Utah's work force. About 300 high-tech firms are located in the state. They employ about 35,000 Utahns. Many of these companies develop and manufacture computer parts and software, military equipment, or spacecraft. Food processing is another leading employer. Foods are canned or frozen at plants in Ogden, Salt Lake City, and Logan.

Some people work in factories that smelt (heat and melt) copper ore. Smelting separates the copper from other parts of the ore. Copper ore is mined at Bingham Canyon, one of the world's largest open-pit mines, near Salt Lake City. Other mines in Utah produce coal. About 1 percent of Utah's workers hold jobs in mining.

Utah is a leading supplier of salt. Workers collect tons of crystals from Great Salt Lake every year, using age-old methods of separating the mineral from seawater.

**Beef cattle graze in Utah near the Wasatch Range.**

Not many of Utah's workers make their living as farmers. Of those who do work in agriculture, most raise livestock, mainly beef cattle, turkeys, and sheep. Utah is a leading sheep-raising state, producing about 4.5 million pounds of wool a year.

**A field of grain spans acres of farmland in northern Utah.**

Most crops are grown in the northern part of the state, where water from rivers and mountain streams is used to irrigate fields and orchards. Major crops include wheat, barley, hay, apricots, cherries, potatoes, and onions.

Utah has a large population of young people. In the years ahead, Utah will have more young people entering the work force than other states will. This is one reason why many growing companies are moving to Utah. These firms see Utah's well-educated youth as a key to future success.

**Computers make learning fun for these students in Utah.**

The prairie dog *(above)* gets its name from its home (the prairie) and from the barking sound it makes when it sees an enemy coming. If a prairie dog spots trouble, it stands tall and barks out a warning cry *(left)*, telling all the dogs to disappear deep into their burrows.

# Protecting the Environment

Utah, like other states, has its share of environmental problems. One problem Utahns are facing is the need to protect wildlife. This need arose long ago, when settlers first tried to earn a living off Utah's land.

The animals of Utah thrived in an unspoiled environment until people began building farms and ranches. At that time, many wild animals had to find new habitats, where they were forced to compete with other animals for food. Some types of animals nearly became extinct.

The Utah prairie dog is one example of a species that came close to extinction. From the story of the prairie dog, Utahns know that the loss of a species can affect the environment. They also know that the animals can be saved.

The Utah prairie dog lives only in Utah. Two hundred years ago, the animal's population probably reached well into the millions. By 1975 only about 5,000 Utah prairie dogs were left.

A prairie dog hardly looks like a poodle or a collie. Instead, this rodent is a relative of the squirrel. Like a squirrel, the prairie dog has a small head and body with short fur.

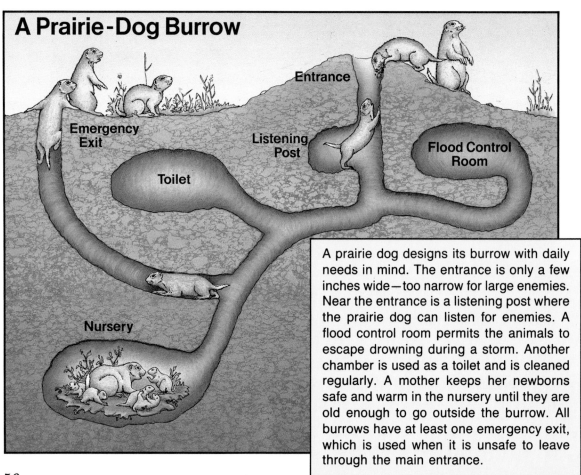

# A Prairie-Dog Burrow

Emergency Exit

Toilet

Entrance

Listening Post

Flood Control Room

Nursery

A prairie dog designs its burrow with daily needs in mind. The entrance is only a few inches wide—too narrow for large enemies. Near the entrance is a listening post where the prairie dog can listen for enemies. A flood control room permits the animals to escape drowning during a storm. Another chamber is used as a toilet and is cleaned regularly. A mother keeps her newborns safe and warm in the nursery until they are old enough to go outside the burrow. All burrows have at least one emergency exit, which is used when it is unsafe to leave through the main entrance.

It also has long claws, which it uses for digging, and two large front teeth. The Utah prairie dog has a white tail. Most other types of prairie dog have black tails.

Utah prairie dogs make their home in south central Utah, where they find plenty of grasses to eat. They dig underground homes called burrows. Hundreds of burrows in one area make up a prairie-dog town.

South central Utah is also home to many livestock farmers. Cattle and sheep graze on the rangelands. When ranchers first started raising livestock in Utah, people looked upon Utah prairie dogs as enemies because they competed with the livestock for grasses to eat.

In the late 1800s, ranchers complained that their livestock did not have enough food because the prairie dogs were eating most of the grass. And horses, cattle, and sheep occasionally broke a leg when they stepped into the openings of the prairie dogs' burrows.

Confident that no enemies are around, a Utah prairie dog enjoys a leisurely meal.

In Utah and in other states, the ranchers asked the government to help control the number of prairie dogs on farmlands. By the early 1900s, state and U.S. government agencies were spreading poison across prairie-dog towns throughout the West. The poison killed much of the prairie-dog population. Before long, some people were be-

When prairie dogs are happy, they sometimes kiss each other by locking their two front teeth together.

ginning to wonder if any of the furry little creatures were left.

Widespread poisoning continued until 1963. In 1968 the Utah prairie dog was added to Utah's endangered species list—a listing of specific kinds of wildlife that are close to extinction.

Some of the poison intended for prairie dogs killed other animals as well. Eagles, badgers, and coyotes that ate the poisoned rodents soon died. Black-footed ferrets, one of the rarest animals in North America, were also poisoned. Ferrets live in burrows along the edges of prairie-dog towns.

Other animals also depend on prairie dogs. During the winter, rattlesnakes, insects, and burrowing owls seek shelter from the cold in abandoned prairie-dog burrows. In areas where all the prairie dogs had been killed, none were around to dig burrows. The other animals had to leave the area in search of winter homes.

Since 1975 the government, once in charge of destroying prairie dogs, has been working to increase the rodent's numbers. In Utah, workers use peanut butter or lettuce to capture prairie dogs that burrow on privately owned farmland. The prairie dogs are then released onto Utah's government-owned land, where they will not disturb the ranchers.

**Much of the land in south central Utah is grassy and good for grazing.**

The program is working. By 1983 the Utah prairie dog was no longer considered endangered. By 1990 the state had increased the number of prairie dogs to 20,000.

Although the rodents are not endangered, they are threatened. A threatened species is one that needs protection to survive. If the transplanted populations of prairie dogs survive and grow on their own, the animal can then be taken off Utah's threatened species list.

Fortunately for Utah prairie dogs, people have learned that changing the environment can hurt wildlife. People also realize that hurting wildlife can change the environment. Now, Utah prairie-dog towns are finding their way back on the map.

A Utah prairie-dog family stands at the entrance to its burrow.

# Utah's Famous People

## ACTORS

**Maude Adams** (1872–1953), born in Salt Lake City, was a leading actress of the theater. Adams, whose real name was Maude Kiskadden, first appeared on stage at the age of nine months, when she had the leading role in *The Lost Child*. She appeared in more than 1,500 performances of *Peter Pan* from 1905 to 1907. Adams starred in many other plays, including *The Little Minister, What Every Woman Knows,* and *Romeo and Juliet.*

▲ ROSEANNE BARR ARNOLD

▲ LORETTA YOUNG

**Roseanne Barr Arnold** (born 1952) is a comedienne from Salt Lake City. She began her career in 1981, performing in stand-up comedy clubs. She stars in her own comedy television series, called "Roseanne."

**Loretta Young** (born 1913) appeared in close to 100 motion pictures during the 1930s and 1940s. In 1947 she won an Academy Award for her leading role in *The Farmer's Daughter*. Young was born in Salt Lake City.

## ATHLETES

**Gene Fullmer** (born 1931) held the title Middleweight Boxing Champion of the World in 1957 and from 1959 to 1962. The boxer was born in West Jordan, Utah.

**Merlin Jay Olsen** (born 1940), athlete, actor, and anchorperson from Logan, Utah, began his professional football career as a defensive tackle with the Los Angeles Rams. From 1962 to 1973, Olsen was known as one of the Fearsome Foursome. He joined NBC Sports in 1977 and in 1982 became a member of the Pro Football Hall of Fame. His acting career includes roles in the television series "Little House on the Prairie" and "Father Murphy."

▲ JOHN MARRIOTT

## BUSINESS LEADERS

**John Willard Marriott** (1900–1985) was born in Marriott, Utah. In 1957 he founded what is now one of the country's largest hotel and restaurant chains, the Marriott Corporation.

◀ JAMES BECKWOURTH

**Jerry Hatten Buss** (born 1933) is a real estate executive from Salt Lake City. He owns two sports teams—the Los Angeles Lakers (basketball) and the Los Angeles Kings (hockey).

## EXPLORERS & FUR TRAPPERS

**James P. Beckwourth** (1798–1867?) was an adventurer of the Wild West. Between 1824 and 1826, Beckwourth trapped animals and dug for gold in Utah. He also explored the region and later wrote about his adventures.

**Jim Bridger** (1804–1881), an explorer, was the first white person to discover Great Salt Lake. When he found the salty lake in 1825, he believed he had reached an ocean.

◀ JIM BRIDGER

63

## INVENTORS

**John Moses Browning** (1855–1926) was a gunsmith from Provo who invented the Winchester repeating rifle, the Colt automatic pistol, and the Browning automatic rifle.

**Nolan Kay Bushnell** (born 1943) invented the first coin-operated video game in 1971. The computer programmer from Ogden was a chairperson of the Atari Corporation.

**Philo Taylor Farnsworth** (1906–1971) began experimenting with television at the age of 15. The electronics whiz gave the first demonstration of television in 1934. Farnsworth was born in Beaver, Utah.

▲ PHILO FARNSWORTH

REVA BECK BOSONE ▶

◀ "BIG BILL" HAYWOOD

## LEADERS

**Reva Beck Bosone** (born 1895) served in the U.S. House of Representatives from 1949 to 1952. She is the first female whom Utahns ever elected to this office.

**William ("Big Bill") Haywood** (1869–1928), born in Salt Lake City, was a labor union organizer. He helped establish the Industrial Workers of the World (IWW) in 1905. Because of his antiwar activities during World War I, he was sentenced to 20 years in jail. To avoid being imprisoned, he fled to Russia.

**Brigham Young** (1801–1877) led a group of Mormons from Nauvoo, Illinois, to Salt Lake Valley in 1847. The religious leader governed the Utah Territory from 1850 to 1858 and helped to establish a strong Mormon community. He died in Salt Lake City, leaving behind 27 wives and 47 children.

BRIGHAM ▶ YOUNG

## MUSICIANS

**Maurice Abravanel** (born 1903) was the conductor and music director of the Utah Symphony from 1947 to 1980. During his 33 years with the group, Abravanel helped make it one of the leading orchestras in the country.

**Donny Osmond** (born 1958) and **Marie Osmond** (born 1959) are singers who were born in Ogden. The brother and sister starred on the television show "Donny and Marie" from 1976 to 1979. Donny began performing with his brothers at the age of 4, and Marie began her career at the age of 7.

◄ DONNY and MARIE OSMOND

## OUTLAW

**Butch Cassidy** (1867–1912), a train robber in the days of the Wild West, was also known as Robert or George Leroy Parker. The motion picture *Butch Cassidy and the Sundance Kid* is based on Cassidy's life story. Cassidy was born in Circleville, Utah.

▲ BUTCH CASSIDY *(far right)*

## WRITERS

**Helen Zeese Papanikolas** (born 1918) has written several books about the settlement of various ethnic groups in Utah. Her works include *Toil and Rage in a New Land* and *Immigrants in Utah*. Papanikolas, of Greek heritage, was born in Carbon County, Utah.

**May Swenson** (1919–1989), from Logan, Utah, won several awards for her poetry. Her collections of poems include *A Case of Spines* and *Half Sun, Half Sleep*.

◄ HELEN ZEESE PAPANIKOLAS

65

# Facts-at-a-Glance

**Nickname:** Beehive State
**Song:** "Utah, We Love Thee"
**Motto:** Industry
**Flower:** sego lily
**Tree:** blue spruce
**Bird:** sea gull

**Population:** 1,776,000 (1990 estimate)
**Rank in population, nationwide:** 35th
**Area:** 84,899 sq mi (219,888 sq km)
**Rank in area, nationwide:** 11th
**Date and ranking of statehood:**
   January 4, 1896, the 45th state
**Capital:** Salt Lake City
**Major cities (and populations\*):**
   Salt Lake City (158,440), Provo (77,480), Ogden (67,490), Orem (61,590)
**U.S. senators:** 2
**U.S. representatives:** 3
**Electoral votes:** 5

\*1986 estimates

**Places to visit:** Beehive House in Salt Lake City, Dinosaur National Monument near Vernal, Gold Hill north of Callao, Great Salt Lake, Hovenweep National Monument in southeastern Utah

**Annual events:** Bryce Canyon Cross-Country Ski Run (Feb.), Moab Jeep Safari (April), Golden Spike Anniversary in Promontory (May), Utah Shakespearean Festival in Cedar City (July), Temple Square Christmas Lighting in Salt Lake City (Nov.)

**Natural resources:** copper, gold, silver, coal, natural gas, petroleum, sand and gravel, oil shale, tar sands, salt, uranium

**Agricultural products:** wheat, barley, hay, apricots, cherries, potatoes, onions, beef, milk, wool

**Manufactured goods:** transportation equipment, food products, printed materials, petroleum and coal products, chemicals, computer parts, spacecraft

ENDANGERED SPECIES
**Mammals**—black-footed ferret, wolf
**Birds**—American peregrine falcon, bald eagle, whooping crane
**Reptiles**—Gila monster, desert tortoise
**Fish**—bonytail chub, woundfin, June sucker, razor-back sucker
**Plants**—autumn buttercup, dwarf bear poppy, San Rafael cactus, toadflax cress, Wright fishhook cactus

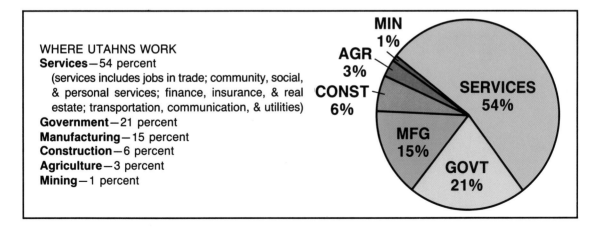

WHERE UTAHNS WORK
**Services**—54 percent
  (services includes jobs in trade; community, social, & personal services; finance, insurance, & real estate; transportation, communication, & utilities)
**Government**—21 percent
**Manufacturing**—15 percent
**Construction**—6 percent
**Agriculture**—3 percent
**Mining**—1 percent

MIN 1%
AGR 3%
CONST 6%
SERVICES 54%
MFG 15%
GOVT 21%

## PRONUNCIATION GUIDE

Deseret (dehz-uh-REHT)

Gila (HEE-luh)

Gosiute (GOH-shoot)

Nauvoo (naw-VOO)

Navajo (NAV-uh-hoh)

Ouray (oo-RAY)

Paiute (PEYE-yoot)

polygyny (puh-LIHJ-uh-nee)

Pueblo (PWEHB-loh)

Shoshone (shuh-SHOHN)

Uinta (yoo-IHN-tuh)

Ute (YOOT)

# Glossary

**canyon**  A narrow valley that has steep, rocky cliffs on its sides.

**desert**  An area of land that receives only about 10 inches (25 cm) or less of rain or snow a year. Some deserts are mountainous; others are expanses of rock, sand, or salt flats.

**immigrant**  A person who moves into a foreign country and settles there.

**inland sea**  A large body of salt water completely surrounded by land and having no outlet.

**irrigation**  Watering land by directing water through canals, ditches, pipes, or sprinklers.

**literacy rate**  A measurement of how many people can read and write.

**plateau**  A large, relatively flat area that stands above the surrounding land.

**polygyny**  The practice of being married to more than one woman at a time.

**pueblo**  Any of the ancient Indian villages in the southwestern United States with buildings of stone or clay, usually built one above the other. The word *Pueblo* also refers to an Indian tribe that lives in the Southwest.

**reservation**  Public land set aside by the government to be used by Native Americans.

**salt flat**  A layer of salt deposits.

**senator**  A member of the Senate, which is one of the two elected groups that make laws for the United States.

**tithe**  One-tenth of a person's income, which is paid to support a church.

**tributary**  A river or stream that feeds, or flows into, a larger river.

# Index ▬▬▬▬▬▬▬▬▬▬▬▬▬▬▬▬▬▬▬▬▬▬▬

**Acknowledgments:**

Maryland Cartographics, Inc., pp. 2, 11; Utah Agricultural Experiment Station, pp. 2–3, 51, 52; Utah Travel Council, pp. 6, 8, 10; Jack Lindstrom, p. 7; Diane Cooper, p. 9; Utah Travel Council/Frank Jensen, pp. 12, 49, 69; Ron Spomer/Visuals Unlimited, p. 13; Louis and Melvina Hitzeman, p. 15; Utah DWR/Jim Weis, p. 16; Utah Department of Natural Resources, pp. 17 (left), 30; Photo by Tony La Gruth (Photo Agent: Jeff Greenberg), p. 17 (right); Doyen Salsig, pp. 18–19, 44, 45; © Crystal Images, 1991, Kathleen Marie Menke, p. 20; National Park Service, p. 21; Thomas Henion, pp. 22, 46; Utah State Historical Society, pp. 23, 25 (inset), 26, 28, 31, 33, 35 (left), 37, 38, 39, 63 (bottom left and bottom right), 64 (top left and top right), 65 (middle and bottom); Church Archives, Church of Jesus Christ of Latter-day Saints, pp. 25, 34, 64 (bottom right); National Cowboy Hall of Fame and Western Heritage Center, p. 29; Smithsonian Institution National Anthropological Archives, Bureau of American Ethnology Collection, Neg. No. 1633, p. 35 (right); Union Station Museum, Ogden, Utah, p. 36 (both); Laura Westlund, pp. 40, 56; Jeff Greenberg, p. 42; Salt Lake Convention and Visitors Bureau, pp. 43, 48, 50; Robert Clayton, pp. 47, 53; © Jerry L. Ferrara, pp. 54 (both), 57, 58, 60, 61; Hollywood Book & Poster Co., pp. 62 (both), 65 (top); Marriott Corp., p. 63 (top); Labor History Archives, Wayne State University, p. 64 (bottom left); Jean Matheny, p. 66; Colin Varga, p. 71.